Ol' Jake's Lucky Day

by ANATOLY IVANOV

Lothrop, Lee & Shepard Books New York

For my friends

Library of Congress Cataloging in Publication Data. Ivanov, Anatoly. Ol' Jake's lucky day. Summary: While Ol' Jake is thinking about how rich he is going to be after he catches and sells a hare he is stalking, the hare runs away into the forest. [1. Hunters—Fiction. 2. Hares—Fiction. 3. Wealth—Fiction] I. Title. PZ7.1934 1984 [E] 83-25645 ISBN 0-688-02866-7 ISBN 0-688-02867-5 (lib. bdg.)

One fine day Ol' Jake spotted a hare.

Today is my lucky day!

I'll catch that hare, Jake whispered.

I'll take it to market and get lots of money for it, and

I'll use the money to buy a pig, which

in no time at all, will have thirteen little piglets.

That hare is as good as caught! Jake thought.

I'll just move in a little closer.

And when my piglets grow up,

they will have their own little piglets.

Soon there will be hundreds of pigs,

and I'll be rich enough to build a house.

My dear wife will be so happy!

And when baby John grows up, I'll make him a fine wedding

with musicians and dancers and kegs and kegs of cider.

The whole village will be green with envy!

I'll spend my old age drinking tea with friends

and watching John oversee the hired hands.

"HEY JOHN! YOU'RE WORKING THE HANDS TOO HARD.
WE WERE POOR FARMERS ONCE!"

Ol' Jake forgot himself and yelled this very loud!

And before he could make another move...

the hare disappeared into the forest,
taking along the pig and hundreds of piglets,

the house, the wedding,
and a whole field full of hired hands!